If Picasso Went to the Sea

By Eric Gibbons

And illustrated by

Art Teachers

If Picasso Went to the Sea

An illustrated introduction to art history for children by art teachers

By Eric Gibbons
Illustrated by art teachers

Image Editing by Dana Ranning
Copy Editing by Sharon Watkins & Paul Rybarczyk
Species Research by Eric Gibbons
Publishing Assistance by Dongkui Lin

ISBN-13: 978-1-940290-55-3
ISBN-10: 1-940290-55-4

Printer: Transcontinental - Printed in Canada
Publisher: Firehouse Publishing: www.firehousepublications.com
Author Website: www.ArtEdGuru.com

Thriving creatures, non-endangered

 Threatened/Vulnerable

 Endangered

 Critically Endangered

 Extinct

More than one shell indicates that some subspecies have different designations.

This book was written and illustrated by art teachers from all over the world who share a passion for art history and education. The author was awarded NJ's Best High School Art Teacher in 2015 by the AENJ. This is the third in the "*If Picasso*" series by the author, preceded by *If Picasso Had A Christmas Tree*, and *If Picasso Went To The Zoo*.

Each teacher has emulated an artist of his/her choosing from history and an alliterative sea creature in a way that honors the work of that artist. By combining art, history, marine biology, and poetry, this book becomes a unique resource for inter-curricular teaching. A combination of art genres is used, from the Renaissance era to modern works, which may bear little resemblance to sea creatures. These art teachers, from elementary level to high school, created these delightful illustrations to share and educate. The contact information for every artist and the author is in the back of this book should you wish to contact them, find out more about their work, or even purchase a print.

We have also uploaded free multi-curricula lesson extensions you can print and share with students of all ages. These lesson extensions are found at www.artedguru.com/ifpicasso.html

Studies show that students who have art succeed at higher rates than their non-art peers. High school students in art outscore their peers by an average of 100 points on the SAT exam. Art makes connections to **all** curricula and promotes creative problem solving. Please support your local art department.

Art makes us smart!

If Pablo Picasso went to the sea,

is this the painting he'd make for me?

This ain't no fish, it's called a porpoise,

cousin to dolphins, they all sing in chorus.

Social by nature they swim with their friends,

migrating with fish, the fun never ends.

This picture you see is called a collage,

cutting and pasting, it is no mirage.

Pablo and Braque invented this style;

we hope that this mammal brings you a smile!

Eric Gibbons, *Pablo Picasso Porpoise,* mixed media collage, 15 x 15 in.

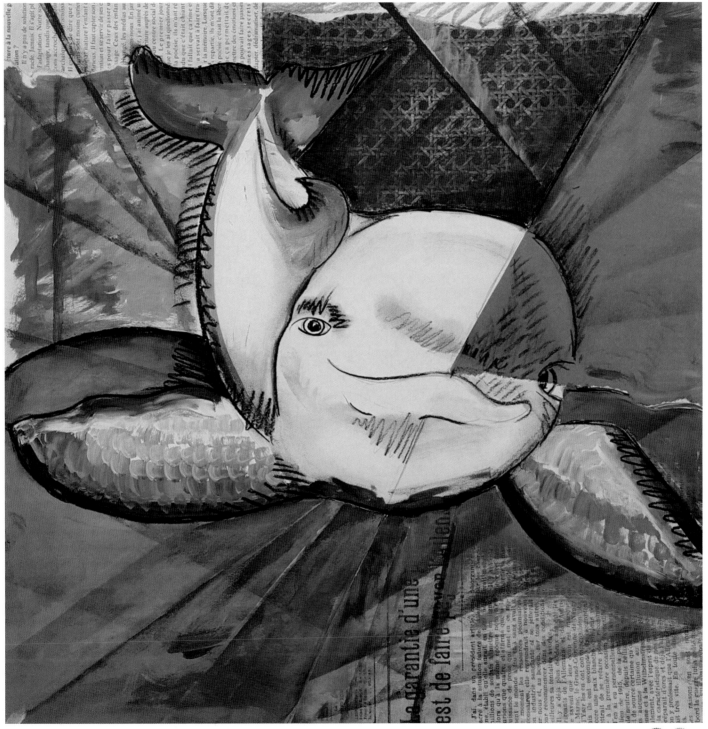

If Edward Hopper went to the sea,

is this the painting he'd make for me?

He was a painter and printmaker too;

he painted all things with a realist view.

H is for horseshoe crab, also for Hopper,

made into *Nightwatch*, it's done very proper.

This crab is so special, a living fossil,

not at all scary, they are very docile.

Go to the beach, perhaps you will see 'em,

or visit a natural history museum.

Chris Hodge, *Edward Hopper Horseshoe Crab*, acrylic on canvas, 10 x 10in.

If Louise Nevelson went to the sea,

is this the sculpture she'd make for me?

Ukranian artist sculpted with wood,

scraps that she found in boxes she glued.

Can you see the Narwhals, Jim, June, and Ned?

They've screws for their horns, and wood for their head.

The horn on a narwhal is really a tusk,

and they hunt for cod from dawn until dusk.

Narwhals are threatened and hunted by men;

if we care for them, they will thrive again.

Lorraine Pulvino Poling, *Louise Nevelson Narwhals*, wood, 12 x 12 in.

If Henri Matisse went to the sea,

is this the collage he'd make for me?

Henry could paint and draw and cut out

all of the things he was thinking about.

Art's more than paintin' to an artful creator;

This manatee made from cut and paste paper.

They are endangered with so precious few,

isn't there something that we can do?

Let's learn about them and their situation,

and find ways to help, and promote conservation.

Julie Kanya, *Henri Matisse Manatee*, paper collage, 10 x 10 in.

13

If Peter Paul Rubens went to the sea,

is this the painting he'd make for me?

Rubens liked painting chubby cheeked folks:

babies, and ladies, and muscular blokes.

A cherub is like a baby with wings,

here with a rosefish he wades and he sings.

Rosefish are boney and not very nice,

they hide and they bite without thinking twice.

This scaly sea creature is found rather deep,

predator fish, they prowl and they creep.

Michelle D. Dillon, *Peter Paul Rubens Rose fish*, oil on canvas, 10 x 10 in.

If Reza Abbasi went to the sea,
is this the painting he'd make for me?
Reza from Persia, now called Iran,
painted for kings, a talented man.
He liked painting small, a miniaturist,
paintings so small, they'd fit on your fist.
Here in this picture an angelfish youth,
sitting so graceful, hardly uncouth.
Angelfish live in reefs by the ocean,
or Amazon rivers with ebb and flow motion.

Mahdi Fanaei, *Reza Abbasi Angelfish*, gouache on canvas, 50 x 70 cm. (digitally altered for square format)

If Henri Rousseau went to the sea,

is this the painting he'd make for me?

No art school for him, his family was poor,

they put him to work when he was just four.

He loved to paint and he loved to draw,

though critics did tease him for painting at all.

He painted lush gardens in his own ways;

this undersea garden includes a few rays.

Cousins to sharks, rays don't just swim,

they fly through the water without a shark's fin.

Chris Hodge, *Henri Rosseau Ray*, acrylic on canvas, 18 x 18 in.

19

If Edward Tingatinga went to the sea,

is this the painting he'd make for me?

Tingatinga is now the name of this style,

started by Edward, he did it a while.

Tourists did love it so very much,

Ed taught Tanzanians to paint it as such.

With spots like a tiger and seaweed behind,

this shark looks pretty, but I must remind,

they are the meanest of any a shark,

hunting alone, and mostly at dark.

Dawn Eaton, *Edward Saidi Tingatinga Tiger Shark*, enamel on board, 12 x 12 in.

If Cy Twombly went to the sea,

is the painting he'd make for me?

Trumpet fish made with a scribbly line,

and blended background that looks like spilled wine.

These fish like to swim with their nose facing down,

and hide in seaweed so as not to be found.

They blend with the coral and grasses down there,

thrive in warm waters, but do so with care,

'cause other sea creatures might like to munch

on trumpet fish sandwich for their daily lunch.

Joy Schultz, *Cy Twombly Trumpet Fish*, acrylic charcoal on canvas, 16 x 29 in.

If Pedro Linares went to the sea,
is this the sculpture he'd make for me?
Mexican artist, born south of U.S.,
invented an art form called alebrijes.
Creatures he made with paper maché,
covered in patterns, for that was his way.
Here is a fish that stands on two feet,
he's called a lookdown, this one's so neat!
From Canadian waters to Uruguay shore,
lookup the lookdown, and learn a bit more.

Shelli Romero, *Pedro Linares Lopez Lookdown Fish*, papier mâché, 12 x 9 x 13.5 in.

If Mary May Morris went to the sea,

is this the embroidery she'd sew for me?

A talented family, many reached fame,

her dad was real famous, Will Morris his name.

She loved to sew and make art with a pin,

flowing designs, with her unique spin.

Man o' war jelly is made like she might;

dangerous creature, though they do not fight.

They float on the water with venomous tail,

and a bubble up top that acts like a sail.

Marie Elcin, *Mary May Morris Man of War*, embroidery, 10 x 10 in.

If Yoshizawa Akira went to the sea,

is this the fish he'd fold for me?

This man of Japan made art from rice paper.

He was the master, no one was greater.

He used origami to teach people math,

but art had become the goal of his path.

Upon this fish's head he carries a dangler,

luring in prey, it's the job of the *angler*.

Found deep below, with pressure above,

he has a face only a mother could love!

Eric Gibbons, *Akira Yoshizawa Anglerfish*, variation on a model by John Montroll, Tyvek paper, 6 x 6 in

If Julia Cameron went to the sea,

is this the photo she'd take for me?

She started her art so late in her life,

and critics unkind did cause her much strife,

but Julia's work was ahead of its time,

now it is treasured, considered sublime.

But not so the fish *chimaera monstrosa*,

so very ugly, please go no close-a.

They live on the bottom where they lay their eggs,

with pectoral fins you might think are legs.

Eric Gibbons, *Julia Margaret Cameron Chimaera Monstrosa*, digital image, 10 x 10 in

31

If Constantin Brâncuși went to the sea,

is this the sculpture he'd make for me?

Romanian artist, working in France,

carved abstract forms, it wasn't by chance.

This barracuda is made very simple,

smooth alabaster, not even a dimple.

Barracudas are long, nearly a snake,

mean like a shark, they won't cut you a break.

With teeth like piranha you should take care,

swimming near reefs, you'll find them there.

Laurel Archambault, *Constantin Brâncuși Barracuda*, alabaster, 11 x 10 x 4 in.

If Minnie Evans went to the sea,

is this the painting she'd make for me?

This lady of color from the southern U.S.,

liked using crayons, and thought them the best.

She painted the dreams she had as a girl.

Did she dream this eel, turned in a curl?

Eels are fish that are very long,

they are not snakes, to say so is wrong.

They come in all sizes, very eclectic,

believe it or not, one is electric!

Ted Edinger, *Minnie Evans Eel*, mixed media, 18 x 18 in.

If Richard Allen went to the sea,

is this the painting he'd make for me?

Allen, op artist, liked painting illusions,

colors and patterns in visual fusions.

This albacore tuna swims in the ocean.

Pink and teal lines give it it's motion.

Tuna are fast, and squid they do eat,

swimming in schools, an undersea fleet.

They are important, a source of nutrition.

Hunting and storing them is our tradition.

Kim Huyler Defibaugh, *Richard Allen Albacore Tuna*, acrylic on canvas, 12 x 12 in.

If Miriam Schapiro went to the sea,
is this the artwork she'd make for me?
She was an artist who pushed for girls rights,
but did it through art, not with fist fights.
She liked to add fabric onto her painting,
her feminist message was so fascinating.
The *sea snail* you see is done in her way;
gastropods carry their shell all the day.
Some snails are big, some small as a bug,
and those without shells are called a sea slug.

Kathy Walthy Rosa, *Miriam Schapiro Sea Snail*, acrylic and fabric on canvas, 36 x 36 in

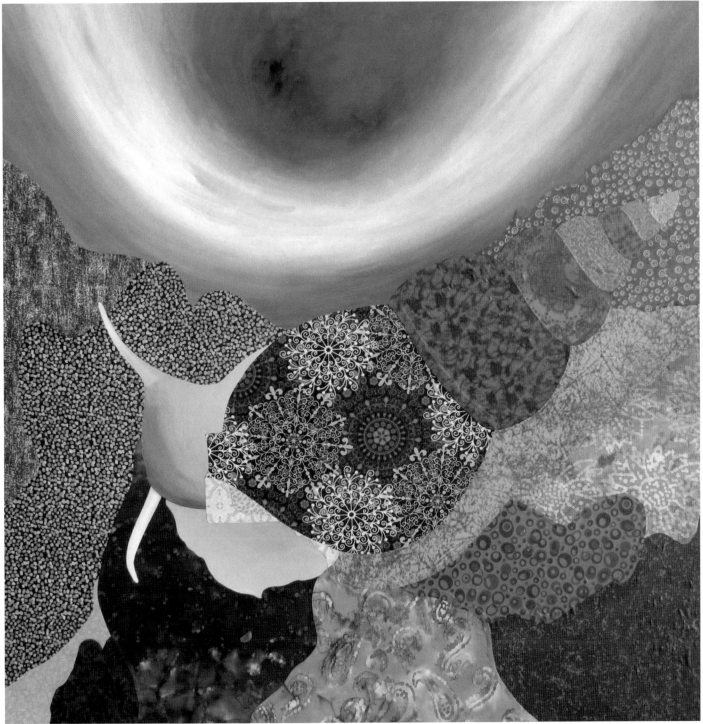

If Mary Edmonia Lewis went to the sea,
is this the sculpture she'd make for me?
This lady of colors was born in New York,
and moved to Europe to continue her work.
She sculpted in marble, a stone that is white;
this leatherback turtle is done like she might.
They eat jellyfish controlling the swarm,
and come to the beach as it gets warm,
to lay all their eggs, as precious as gold,
hatching when they are near sixty days old.

Eric Gibbons, *Mary Edmonia Lewis Leatherback Turtle*, plaster, 15 x 15 x 8 in.

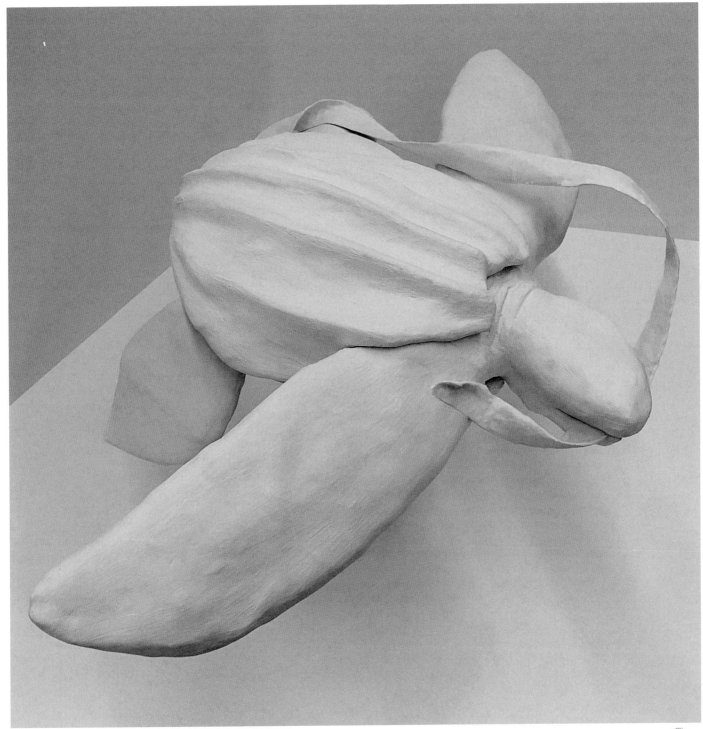

If André Derain went to the sea,

is this the painting he'd make for me?

He was a fauvist, a friend to Matisse;

both used wild colors, wild as beasts.

André used color to express his views.

This dragonet fish is done with bold hues.

Sandy sea bottoms are where these fish lay,

cousin to goby's, or so experts say.

Some "little dragons" don't even have scales,

and some carry venom from head to their tails.

Cindy Erickson, *André Derain Dragonet Fish*, oil pastel, 11 x 14 in.

43

If Nakahara Nantenbô went to the sea,

is this the painting he'd make for me?

Samurai ancestors, and master of Zen,

he painted with ink on paper back then.

Here is a nautilus done in his way,

with a swirl, and a splash, in black, white, and gray.

Nautilus live in a shell that they build,

for mollusks make shells, they are so skilled.

Since dinosaur times they've been around,

we know this from fossils they've left in the ground.

Eric Gibbons, *Nakahara Nantenbô Nautilus*, ink on paper, 14 x 14 in.

45

If Erté the artist went to the sea,
is this the painting he'd make for me?
Russian by birth, master of all,
from painting to jewelry, to gowns for the ball!
With lines that are graceful and colors so bold,
his work was a treasure to have and behold.
This emperor shrimp is shown like he might,
upon a seahorse, looks ready to fight.
With sea cucumbers they partner and eat,
one helps the other, no need to compete.

K. Erica Dodge, *Erté Emperor Shrimp*, gouache, 16 x 16 in.

If William Blake went to the sea,

is this the painting he'd make for me?

Printmaker, painter, and even a poet,

London his home, perhaps you may know it.

The blowfish you see here to the right,

is done in a way that Mr. Blake might.

Puffers are toxic, a poisonous fish,

Japanese serve them, a specialty dish.

When they are frightened they puff very large,

stopping a predator's hunger-filled charge.

Heather Lass, *William Blake Blowfish*, acrylic colored pencil on canvas, 12 x 14 in.

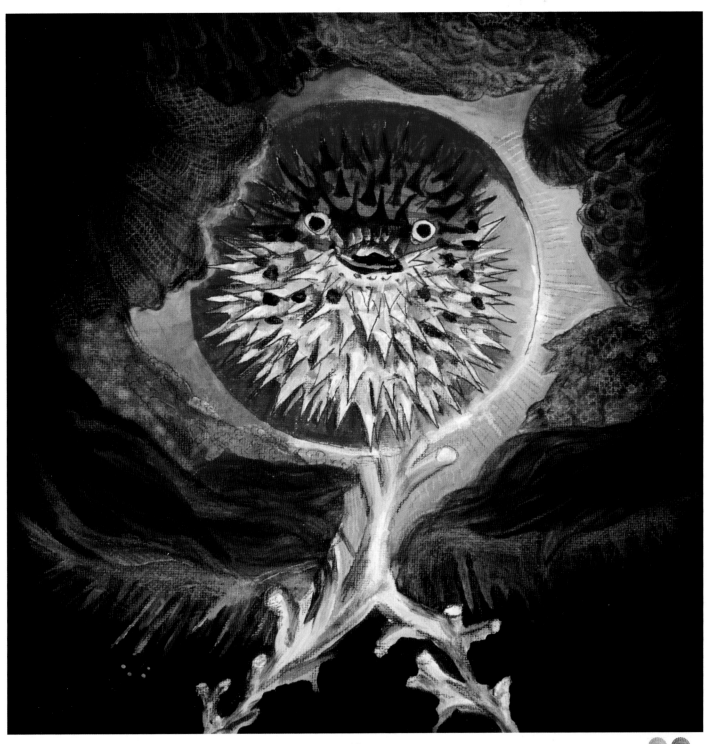

If Élisabeth Sonrel went to the sea,
is this the painting she'd make for me?
France was her home and Nouveau was her style,
with intertwined lines that flowed like the Nile.
Sea nettles are jellies, but this jelly stings
with poisonous cells that hide in their strings
that flow from their bell, that opens and closes,
pretty like flowers and thorns like some roses.
They flow with warm currents and dive rather deep,
as tentacles follow, for food they do sweep.

Michele Lindsey Andrade, *Élisabeth Sonrel Sea Nettles*, acrylic on canvas, 12 x 12 in.

51

If Frida Kahlo went to the sea,

is this the painting she'd make for me?

This Mexican lady painted her face,

dream-like and haunting, a surreal space.

The krill on her shoulders give her a kiss,

while she stares ahead as if nothing's amiss.

Krill are quite tiny crustaceans you'll know,

food for the whales away deep below.

And krill eat the plankton, smaller than sand,

the circle of life is ever so grand!

Vivianna Acuña-Francisco, *Frida Kahlo Krill*, oil on canvas, 30 x 30 in.

If Sasaki Chojiro went to the sea,

is this the raku he'd make for me?

Raku is a method of working with clay,

invented by Chojiro, done in a Zen way.

Co-scin-o-dis-cus are smaller than sand,

algae in oceans, and puddles on land.

They are just one of a family of cells,

diatoms are their name, they're tiny shells.

A microscope's needed in order to see 'em,

one tiny drop contains a museum!

Julie Bousum, *Sasaki Chojiro Coscinodiscus*, raku fired clay, 12 x 12 in.

If George Rouault went to the sea,

is this the painting he'd make for me?

Expressionist artists paint with their feeling,

for them the whole process is very healing.

From a poor family, in Paris the city,

his paintings were rough and not always pretty.

These fish have masks, as round as a dish,

for this is the *raccoon butterfly fish*.

As big as your hand if you open it wide,

within coral reefs they tend to reside.

Annie Thomas-Eyster, *Georges Rouault Raccoon Butterfly fish*, acrylic, 16 x 16 in.

If Gustav Klimt went to the sea,

is this the painting he'd make for me?

Koi are gold fish with whiskers like mice,

treasured in Asia in gardens so nice.

Sometimes called carp with many a hue,

they can be black, white, red, and rare blue.

Did you know they eat baby mosquitoes,

not burgers or fries or tasty burritos?

Klimt loved to paint with colors and gold,

and patterns throughout—his style so bold.

Rachel Wintemberg, *Gustav Klimt Koi*, acrylic on masonite, 15 x 15 in.

If Hildegard of Bingen went to the sea,

is this the painting she'd make for me?

This German woman, considered a saint,

was known for her writing, and things she did paint.

She loved to use patterns, mostly in circles,

these are detailed in her many journals.

The halibut here has two eyes on one side,

they lie in the sand in order to hide.

Both eyes poking up they are very shrewd,

'cause they are the sea's most popular food.

Ashley M Gonzalez, *Hildegard of Bingen Halibut*, watercolor and mixed media on paper, 19 x 19 ▶

61

If Beatrice Wood went to the sea,

is this the clay form she'd sculpt for me?

American artist, a potter by trade,

known for metallic ceramics she made.

This one is done with a pair of sea dragons,

but not like the ones fought by Billy Bo Baggins.

Weedy sea dragons are cousins you'd guess,

of tiny seahorses, but I do digress.

They hide in seaweed off the coast of Australia,

covered in finny-fin paraphernalia.

Connie Berger, *Beatrice Wood Weedy Sea Dragon*, ceramic, 6.5 x 8 in.

If Camille Pissarro went to the sea,

is this the painting he'd make for me?

Camille was a mentor to painters in France,

Impressionism the way their brushes danced.

Paint put on canvas was bold and so thick,

to paint what they saw, this was their kick.

The plankton we see in this textured work,

are quite microscopic, they drift and they lurk.

Some light up bright at night in the bay,

and make easy-pickins for their hungry prey.

Shawny Montgomery, *Camille Pissarro Plankton*, acrylic on canvas, 12 x 12 in.

If Janet Sobel went to the sea,

is this the painting she'd make for me?

Janet liked dripping and splashing her paint,

expressively painting, she had no restraint.

Her style of dripping was echoed by Pollock,

if she painted salmon, she'd capture their frolic.

With waves of bold color, that splash like the waters,

this may be why she was copied by others.

Spawn in the rivers, then swim to the sea,

salmon returning, life's circle is key.

Diane Stinebaugh, *Janet Sobel Salmon*, acrylic on canvas, 18 x 18 in.

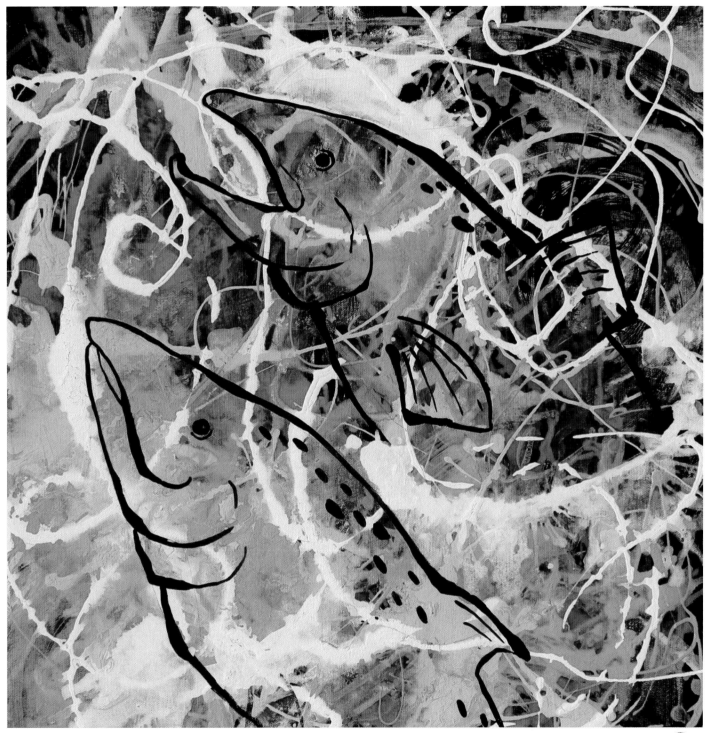

If Hanns Scharff went to the sea,

is this the mosaic he'd make for me?

Artist of tiles, a true innovator,

once held the job of an interrogator!

Here in his style, a gorgeous seahorse,

made up of shards, mosaic of course.

Bony seahorses have another odd name,

that's hippocampus of mythical fame.

And though we know horses are very tall,

tropic sea horses are really quite small.

Leah Keller, *Hanns Scharff Seahorse*, ceramic mosaic, 30 x 30 in.

If Oscar Howe went to the sea,
is this the painting he'd make for me?
Dakota his tribe, descended from chiefs,
his art was his life and contained his beliefs.
This Sioux painting style was focused on lines,
merged man and earth's creatures almost like signs,
with flat and bold color, can you see them here?
Hammerhead sharks like warm waters my dear,
and gather together in groups called a school,
but hunting at night, alone is the rule.

Nicole Horgan, *Oscar Howe Hammerhead Shark*, digital media, 10 x 10 in.

71

If Georgia O'Keeffe went to the sea,

is this the painting she'd make for me?

Georgia is famous for her giant flowers,

but she painted mountains, and big city towers.

She'd make thing look big by zooming in;

these octopus legs are done with her spin.

Octopi creatures are so very smart,

undersea ninjas, it's almost an art.

They sometimes change color called camouflage,

hiding by matching, a kind of mirage.

Deborah W. Pey, *Georgia O'Keeffe Octopus*, acrylic on paper, 16 x 16 in.

If René Magritte went to the sea,

is this the painting he'd make for me?

René was a Belgian surrealist painter,

pictures so dreamlike, a true entertainer.

This is a fish, we call it a molly,

covered in clouds, it's so very jolly.

This freshwater fish from rivers and stream,

mostly in Mexico, so it does seem.

Often the molly, like goldfish are pets,

but mollies are meaner; bullies, not guests.

Victoria Smith, *René Magritte Molly*, acrylic on canvas, 24 x 24 in.

If Margaret Mackintosh went to the sea,

is this the painting she'd make for me?

Glasgow her style flowed with such grace,

with Celtic long lines that fill up the space.

Mollusks are critters that build their own home,

a shell on their backs wherever they roam.

If you count sea creatures, and put them in order,

the shell bearing ones make nearly a quarter

of all that's down under the sleepy blue ocean,

eating, and playing, and swimming in motion.

Katie Kasberg, *Margaret Macdonald Mackintosh Mollusk*, mixed media, 12 x 12 in.

If Roy Lichtenstein went to the sea,

is this the painting he'd make for me?

Roy, a pop artist, loved his bold hues,

heavy outlines that he liked to use.

Here is a lobster crawling along

the sandy sea floor, it's where he belongs.

Crustacean he is, along with his friends,

shells on outside on this they depend.

If you ask them why, don't be too hasty,

for you'd need a shell if you were so tasty!

Mary Jane Coker, *Roy Lichtenstein Lobster*, acrylic on paper, 10 x 10 in.

If Vincent van Gogh went to the sea,

is this the painting he'd make for me?

Do you know this creature, the Vampire Squid?

The tropical ocean is where he is hid.

The skin 'tween his legs looks like a bat,

he swims very deep, and hard to look at.

Don't worry yourself, it's unlikely you'll see him,

even if you go for very deep swimmin'.

Like Vincent this creature is misunderstood,

what sometimes seems ugly can be very good.

Daryn P. Martin, *Vincent van Gogh Vampire Squid*, acrylic on canvas, 12 x 12 in.

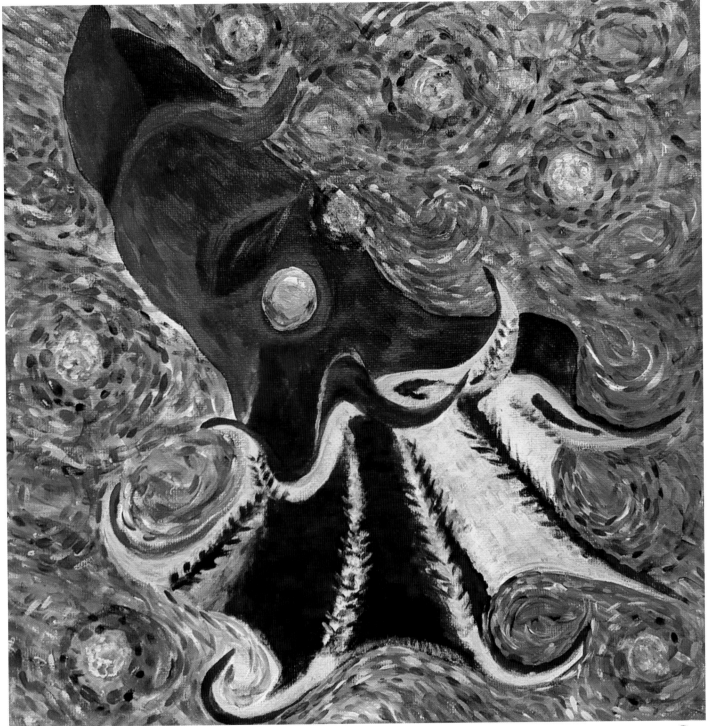

If Robert Rauschenberg went to the sea,
is this the collage he'd make for me?
Rob, a pop artist would use what he found,
pictures from books and junk on the ground.
Collage is collecting and making it art,
recycling stuff can be the best part.
Remora are fish that like to hitch rides,
like on a turtle or on a shark's sides.
Their head has a sucker that helps them hold on,
so they can relax from dusk until dawn.

Eric Gibbons, *Robert Rauschenberg Remora*, mixed media collage, 11 x 11 in.

If Sandro Botticelli went to the sea,
is this the painting he'd make for me?
This Renaissance artist worked for the Pope,
mythical images, art filled with hope.
Here in this picture we see a white whale,
standing upright, upon her long tail.
Belugas, toothed whales, swim in the north,
within icy waters they often set forth,
hunting for fish, be it salmon or cod;
social by nature, they swim in a pod.

Kathy Carruba Schmidt, *Sandro Botticelli Beluga Whale*, acrylic on canvas, 20 x 20 in.

If Rembrandt van Rijn went to the sea,

is this the painting he'd make for me?

Known for his portraits done in Baroque,

he'd paint himself and his neighborly folk.

Darkened backgrounds and eyes full of soul,

grandest of masters the experts extol.

This rockfish is done in his earthen hue.

Did you know some live to two hundred and two?

These carnivore fish like to eat meat,

swimming as deep as ten-thousand feet!

Connie L. McClure, *Rembrandt Chesapeake Bay Rockfish*, oil on canvas, 10 x 10 in.

If Willem de Kooning went to the sea,

is this the painting he'd make for me?

Scrubbing and dripping, it looks rather wild;

can you see the dolphin that's hidden inside?

Mammals they are, and full of affection,

if sharks are around, they'll offer protection.

But we've let them down, our actions are linked,

For some river dolphins are nearly extinct!

Caring for creatures takes more than compassion,

we hope that this book encourages action.

Eric Gibbons, *Willem de Kooning Dolphin*, acrylic on canvas, 30 x 30 in.

If Georges Seurat went to the sea,

is this the painting he'd make for me?

The interesting thing about Mr. Seurat,

is he liked to paint by just using the dot.

This pointillist painting of a sea otter,

has an umbrella while floating on water.

Making their homes in the northern Pacific,

social sea mammals are really terrific.

It's rare to behold them, threatened by strangers

so rare in fact, they're considered endangered.

Kelly Henrikson, *Georges Seurat Sea Otter*, acrylic on canvas, 10 x 10 in.

If Ernst Haeckel went to the sea,

is this the image he'd make for me?

German biologist, Darwin his friend,

many a creature discovered and penned.

Drawing them all as pictures in books,

these hydrae are done with similar looks.

Hydrae are tiny, less than an inch,

and they have a stinger that surely will pinch.

Weirdest of all, if they lose an arm,

it will grow back, and causes no harm!

LaDawna Dillman, *Ernst Haeckel Hydrae*, pen and ink on paper, 11 x 11 in.

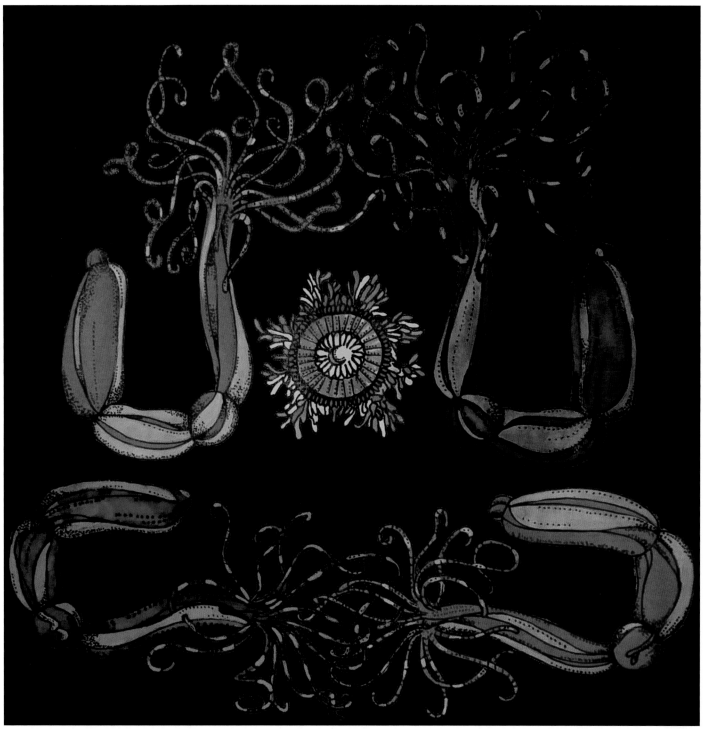

If Marisol Escobar went to the sea,

is this the sculpture she'd make for me?

Some artists so famous are known by one name,

Picasso, Matisse, Marisol had such fame.

This Latin lady assembled her art,

wood, and some patterns, and paint were her start.

She's put them together like this marlin fish,

to make it pop art, for that was her wish.

Marlins can swim as fast as a car,

hunters like sharks, but faster by far.

Marie Elcin, *Marisol Escobar Marlin*, carved and painted found wood, 8 x 3 x 5 in

If Katsushika Hokusai went to the sea,

is this the print he'd make for me?

Printing from wood he did in Japan,

a master of ukiuo-e, a Tokyo man.

This is his wave with a big humpback whale,

thirty-nine tons, surely breaking a scale!

Found in the ocean and seas 'round the globe,

they travel for miles and live on microbes.

Once they were hunted then nearly all gone,

With conservation, now thrive and live on.

If Alexander Calder went to the sea,

is this the sculpture he'd make for me?

The mobile as sculpture was his invention,

it moves in the wind in every direction.

Clams on this mobile are red, black, and white,

balancing bivalvia, a delightful sight.

Clams come in many colors and sizes,

but some clams are dying as temperature rises.

Do what you can to care for the seas,

sharing and caring is what this world needs.

Eric Gibbons, *Alexander Calder Clams*, mixed media, 10 x 16 x 10 in.

7: Eric Gibbons
Pablo Picasso Porpoise
www.artedguru.com
www.firehousepublications.com

19: Chris Hodge
Henri Rosseau Ray
www.chodgeart.com
diebox1984-art@yahoo.com

9: Chris Hodge
Edward Hopper Horseshoe Crab
www.chodgeart.com
diebox1984-art@yahoo.com

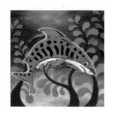

21: Dawn Eaton
Edward Tingatinga Tiger Shark
www.dawneaton.com

11: Lorraine Pulvino Poling
Louise Nevelson Narwhals
elseapea@yahoo.com

23: Joy Schultz
Cy Twombly Trumpet Fish
joyschult2@gmail.com
schultzjoy.wordpress.com

13: Julie Kanya
Henri Matisse Manatee
Aerosmithgirl71@gmail.com

25: Shelli Romero
Pedro Lopez Lookdown Fish
romeroshelli@gmail.com

15: Michelle D. Dillon
Peter Paul Rubens Rose fish
mddillon1@verizon.net
www.mddillon.com

27: Marie Elcin
Mary May Morris Man of War
marieelcin@hotmail.com
www.colored-thread.blogspot.com

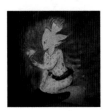

17: Mahdi Fanaei
Reza Abbasi Angelfish
MahdiFanaei@gmail.com
Fanaei.mihanblog.com

29: Eric Gibbons
Akira Yoshizawa Anglerfish
www.artedguru.com
www.firehousepublications.com

31: Eric Gibbons
Julia Cameron Chimaera Monstrosa
www.artedguru.com
www.firehousepublications.com

43: Cindy Erickson
André Derain Dragonet Fish
erickson16@cox.net

33: Laurel Archambault
Constantin Brâncuși Barracuda
laurelarchambault@hotmail.com
laurelarchambault.wix.com/artist

45: Eric Gibbons
Nakahara Nantenbô Nautilus
www.artedguru.com
www.firehousepublications.com

35: Ted Edinger
Minnie Evans Eel
tededinger@gmail.com
www.artwithmre.com

47: K. Erica Dodge
Erté Emperor Shrimp
erica_ddg@yahoo.com

37: Kim Huyler Defibaugh
Richard Allen Albacore Tuna
drkimbeg@cox.net

49: Heather Lass
William Blake Blowfish
lassartwork@gmail.com

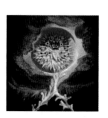

39: Kathy Walthy Rosa
Miriam Schapiro Sea Snail
bostondogs@live.com

51: Michele Lindsey Andrade
Élisabeth Sonrel Sea Nettles
MLAndrade8@yahoo.com

41: Eric Gibbons
Mary Edmonia Lewis Leatherback Turtle
www.artedguru.com
www.firehousepublications.com

53: Vivianna Acuña-Francisco
Frida Kahlo Krill
vivianna@vivianna.org

55: Julie Bousum
Sasaki Chojiro Coscinodiscus
jkbousum@aol.com

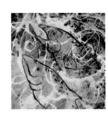

67: Diane Stinebaugh
Janet Sobel Salmon
dianeadams14@gmail.com

57: Annie Thomas-Eyster
Georges Rouault Raccoon Butterfly fish
aeyster@edon-nw.org

69: Leah Keller
Hanns Scharff Seahorse
leeack080969@gmail.com

59: Rachel Wintemberg
Gustav Klimt Koi
thehelpfulartteacher@gmail.com
thehelpfulartteacher.blogspot.com

71: Nicole Horgan
Oscar Howe Hammerhead Shark
Nicolecatherinerose@outlook.com

61: Ashley M Gonzalez
Hildegard of Bingen Halibut
arushatz13@hotmail.com
themagnificentpaintbrush.blogspot.com

73: Deborah W. Pey
Georgia O'Keeffe Octopus
debpey@aol.com

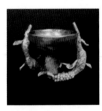

63: Connie Berger
Beatrice Wood Weedy Sea Dragon
Connieberger@gmail.com

75: Victoria Smith
Rene Magritte Molly
Vks84@aol.com

65: Shawny Montgomery
Camille Pissarro Plankton
shawnymonty@gmail.com

77: Katie Kasberg
Margaret Mackintosh Mollusk
katiekasberg@yahoo.com

79: Mary Jane Coker
Roy Lichtenstein Lobster
meejean@bellsouth.net

91: Kelly Henrikson
Georges Seurat Sea Otter
kel624@gmail.com

81: Daryn P. Martin
Vincent van Gogh Vampire Squid
darynpmartin@gmail.com

93: LaDawna Dillman
Ernst Haeckel Hydra
kindofabigdillart@gmail.com

83: Eric Gibbons
Robert Rauschenberg Remora
www.artedguru.com
www.firehousepublications.com

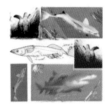

95: Marie Elcin
Marisol Escobar Marlin
marieelcin@hotmail.com
www.colored-thread.blogspot.com

85: Kathy Carruba Schmidt
Sandro Botticelli Beluga Whale
KathyCSchmidt@gmail.com

97: Eric Gibbons
Hokusai Humpback Whale
www.artedguru.com
www.firehousepublications.com

87: Connie L. McClure,
Rembrandt Chesapeake Bay
connielmcclure@aol.com

99: Eric Gibbons
Alexander Calder Clams
www.artedguru.com
www.firehousepublications.com

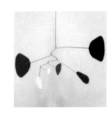

89: Eric Gibbons
Willem de Kooning Dolphin
www.artedguru.com
www.firehousepublications.com

Check out our previous books in the *If Picasso* series.

Many free lesson ideas and hand-outs at:
www.artedguru.com/ifpicasso.html

More great books and resources at www.FirehousePublications.com